Space Quest
Mission to Mars

By Peter Lock

LONDON, NEW YORK, MUNICH,
MELBOURNE, AND DELHI

DK LONDON
Series Editor Deborah Lock
Project Art Editor Ann Cannings
Producers, Pre-production
Francesca Wardell, Vikki Nousiainen

Reading Consultant
Shirley Bickler

DK DELHI
Editor Pomona Zaheer
Assistant Art Editor Yamini Panwar
DTP Designers Anita Yadav, Vijay Kandwal
Picture Researcher Surya Sarangi
Deputy Managing Editor Soma B. Chowdhury

First published in Great Britain by
Dorling Kindersley Limited
80 Strand, London, WC2R 0RL

Copyright © 2014 Dorling Kindersley Limited
A Penguin Random House Company
10 9 8 7 6 5 4 3 2 1
001—195868—June/2014

A CIP catalogue record for this book
is available from the British Library
ISBN: 978-1-4093-5193-1

Printed and bound in China by South China Printing Company.

The publisher would like to thank the following for their kind permission
to reproduce their photographs:
(Key: a-above; b-below/bottom; c-centre; f-far; l-left; r-right; t-top)
1 Getty Images: Stocktrek RF. **4–5 NASA:** CXC/JPL-Caltech/STScI (Background). **6 Science Photo Library:**
Roger Harris (cl). **6–7 NASA:** CXC/JPL-Caltech/STScI. **7 NASA:** JPL (c). **8–61 NASA:** ESA and G. Bacon (STScI) (b).
8 NASA: (t). **9 NASA:** Jim Grossmann (b). **10 Dreamstime.com:** Julien Tromeur (tl). **11 NASA:** Jack Pfaller.
13 Dreamstime.com: Julien Tromeur (br). **NASA:** (c). **15 NASA:** MSFC (c). **16 NASA:** (tl).**16–17 Alamy Images:**
NASA Images (c). **NASA:** CXC/JPL-Caltech/STScI. **18 NASA:** JPL (t). **19 NASA:** (t). **21 Dreamstime.com:**
Alexokokok (c/Frame). **Science Photo Library:** Roger Harris (c). **22 Dreamstime.com:** Julien Tromeur (bl). **23 NASA:** (t).
25 Dreamstime.com: Alexokokok (tc/Frame). **NASA:** ESA, and the Hubble Heritage Team (STScI/AURA) (tc).
26–27 Fotolia: Derya Celik (Scrolls). **NASA:** CXC/JPL-Caltech/STScI. **27 Alamy Images:** Gianni Dagli Orti/The Art
Archive (r). **28 NASA:** JPL-Caltech (t). **29 NASA:** (c). **31 NASA:** JPL-Caltech (t). **32 NASA:** JPL-Caltech (t).
35 NASA: JPL-Caltech (t). **36 ESA:** DLR/FU Berlin (b). **36–37 NASA:** CXC/JPL-Caltech/STScI. **37 NASA:**
JPL-Caltech (c). **38–39 NASA:** CXC/JPL-Caltech/STScI. **38–89 Science Photo Library:** Chris Butler (c). **40 NASA:**
JPL-Caltech/MSSS (t). **41 Dreamstime.com:** Julien Tromeur (br). **42–43 NASA:** JPL/Arizona State University (t).
44–45 Corbis: Michael Freeman (t). **47 Corbis:** Tony Gervis/Robert Harding World Imagery (t). **48–49 Corbis:** Barry Lewis/
In Pictures (t). **50–51 NASA:** CXC/JPL-Caltech/STScI. **53 NASA:** SDO (tc). **54 Dreamstime.com:** Julien Tromeur.
55 Corbis: Kage-Mikrofotografie/Doc-Stock (tc). **Dreamstime.com:** Alexokokok (tc/Frame). **56–57 NASA:**
JPL-Caltech (t). **57 Dreamstime.com:** Julien Tromeur (tr). **59 NASA:** (t).
Jacket images: Front: Dreamstime.com: Jochen Schönfeld/Time123 (tc); **Fotolia:** victorhabbick (b);
Back: NASA: JPL-Caltech (tl), MOLA Science Team/O. de Goursac, Adrian Lark (cr);
Spine: NASA: MOLA Science Team/O. de Goursac, Adrian Lark (b)

All other images © Dorling Kindersley
For further information see: www.dkimages.com

Discover more at
www.dk.com

Contents

Year 2050 Mission Statement

To visit the planets of the solar system to collect samples, to test experiments and to set up life-supporting bases if possible.

First stage to Mars – 250 days

Order of planets from the Sun:

Mercury
Venus
Earth
Mars
Jupiter
Saturn
Uranus
Neptune

Asteroid belt

Mission team

Name	Age	Role
Ned Crater	41	Commander
Flo Comet	32	Engineer
Alex Nova	35	Lander pilot
Izzy Stardust	29	Science officer
Lem Cosmos	28	Engineer
Coconut	3	Pet rabbit

Planning Space Quest

For 15 years, scientists have been planning Space Quest. This mission has involved careful planning to prepare for possible events.

The spacecraft *Ramesses* has been built section by section in the Earth's outer atmosphere. The astronauts will reach *Ramesses* in a rocket.

Technical data
Ramesses is designed to transport the astronauts through the solar system. Separate landers, such as *Memphis*, have been specially designed for exploring each planet. These have been interlocked with *Ramesses*.

Five years training

The five astronauts have been through intensive training for life in space and to prepare them for each planet's different environment and dangers.

Across the solar system

The first stage is to visit Mars. Afterwards through the asteroid belt to Jupiter and then a sling shot around the Sun to reach Saturn and the outer planets. Refuelling stores have already been sent out across the solar system for *Ramesses* to intercept.

Launch Day

The doors of the lift closed
as the astronauts gave their
last wave to the ground crew.
The lift went up the launch tower
smoothly. The vast gleaming
rocket ready for launch loomed
in front of them.

The ground crew below looked
like ants as they climbed into

their vans and drove to Mission Control. The astronauts wondered how long it would be before they saw those people again. How long would this mission across the solar system last? Would they ever return?

The lift doors opened. Ahead of them was the hatch door to the crew's command capsule at the top of the rocket.

"Give us a smile," said one of the ASPs with a camera.

Ned, Izzy, Alex, Flo and Lem turned at the hatch opening for the final photograph.

They were all kitted out in their orange launch suits, holding their helmets.

The ASPs helped the astronauts
put on their helmets.

"That's a great photo for
the newspapers," said an ASP.

One by one, the astronauts crawled into the capsule on their hands and knees. Everything inside the capsule was tilted 90 degrees. They wriggled in along the back wall and then lifted their legs over their heads to slide into their seats.

As the ASPs harnessed them into their seats, the astronauts focused on the mission ahead. Ned switched on the radio to speak to the CapCom at Mission Control.

"How are the safety checks going?" asked Ned.

"All systems are looking good," replied the CapCom.

CapCom is for Capsule or Spacecraft Communicator. This is the only person who speaks with the astronauts.

"All strapped in," said the ASPs, giving the thumbs up as they crawled out of the capsule. "Good luck, guys!"

The hatch doors closed and the astronauts were left on their own.

A while later, the CapCom spoke, "We're ready to start the countdown!"

The rocket began to vibrate as the liquid-fuelled engines fired up.

"This ride will be better than any rollercoaster," laughed Alex. "Hold tight!"

In Mission Control, the final rapid computer check showed everything was okay.

CapCom said, "All systems are go!"

The rocket engines rumbled.

◀ Launch suit
This one-piece suit has its own oxygen supply. These suits are worn for take off from and returning to Earth.

Outer flame-resistant materials

Heating in boots to protect feet from the cold

Inner cooling materials

Space Suit Design

Whether taking off, exploring planets or taking space walks, each space suit is cleverly designed for each situation an astronaut may encounter.

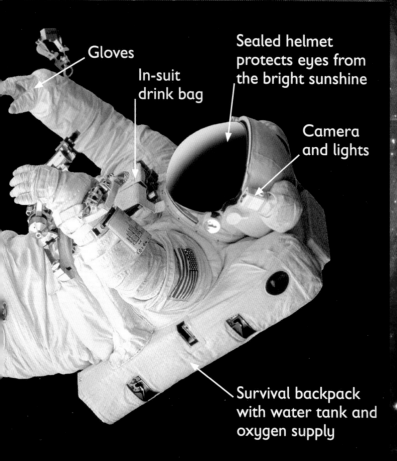

Gloves

In-suit
drink bag

Sealed helmet
protects eyes from
the bright sunshine

Camera
and lights

Survival backpack
with water tank and
oxygen supply

⌃ Life-supporting suit

Astronauts would not be able to survive in
space if it wasn't for the life support provided
in the suit. The suit looks puffed up because
it's full of air. A suit takes over an hour to get
into and astronauts may need a helper.

Life in Space

"We have lift-off," said CapCom.

The rocket zoomed upwards. Jets of fire and billows of smoke blazed behind. The capsule shook violently as did the astronauts' bodies. Their vision blurred.

In the hold, Coconut the rabbit lay curled up, resting in her special space hutch. She opened one eye, stirred and then snuggled up again. This shaking was just like all the launch tests.

The rocket zoomed through the atmosphere. The launch engines dropped away.

As it entered outer space, the rocket levelled out. It sped towards the spacecraft *Ramesses*.

"Look guys! *Ramesses* is fantastic," said Flo, looking at the spacecraft ahead.

Ned took over the rocket's controls as they came close. He steered the rocket towards the docking hatch.

"Great bit of steering, Ned," said Lem, as the rocket slid gently into the dock.

Ned pressed the switch to shut down the rocket's engines.

"Welcome to your new home!" said Ned.

Alex unlocked the hatch and they all wriggled out. They helped each other out of their suits.

"At last!" said Lem. "Let's go and explore."

They floated through the craft. In space, there was less gravity to keep them down.

Alex went to the kitchen area. He flicked through the selection of freeze-dried foods.

Hot or cold water can be added to **dried food** to make some great meals. Washing up is done with special wipes.

"I'm hungry," he thought. Then
he spotted the one he wanted.
"Ice cream – my favourite!"

Izzy went to check on Coconut.

"Her life-support systems show
she is okay," she reported.

Flo went to the exercise area. She strapped herself onto the treadmill.

"I needed this stretch after being cooped up in that capsule," she thought.

Lem was in the sleeping area, strumming his guitar.

"This is a great way to chill out after all that shaking," he thought.

Meanwhile, Ned was at the spacecraft's controls. *Ramesses* was now cruising through space, heading away from Earth towards Mars.

"Look out of a window, guys!" said Ned through the sound system. "A comet is passing on the left side."

"Awesome!" said Izzy. "Let's hope that's a good sign for our mission."

Who was Mars?

The ancient Romans named the planet Mars. The planet looked like a bright red star. The colour reminded them of blood spilled in battle. So they called this planet after their war god, Mars.

The month of March was also named after this god. This was when the Roman war campaigns started again after winter.

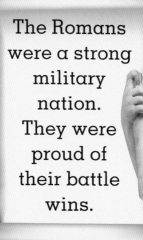

The Romans were a strong military nation. They were proud of their battle wins.

In the Roman myth, Mars was the father of Romulus and Remus – the twins who built Rome.

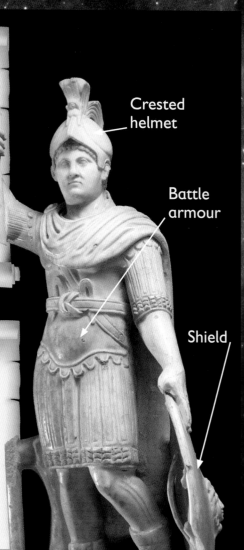

Crested helmet

Battle armour

Shield

Mars Phase 1
Landing

After seven months travelling in space, *Ramesses* reached the outer atmosphere of Mars.

"We're now in orbit around Mars," announced Ned to CapCom. "We should be ready to go for the landing capsule launch soon."

Flo was helping Alex, Lem and Izzy get into their suits for Mars.

"These boots will keep our feet cosy from the Martian cold," said Lem. He pulled on the boots with heated soles.

Once ready, they opened the hatch door and walked into the Mars lander, *Memphis*.

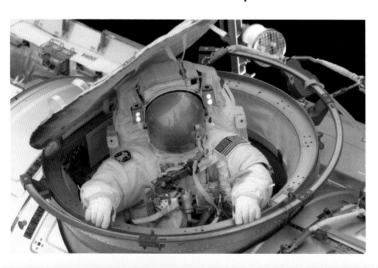

"Good luck," said Flo, waving them goodbye as she closed the hatch. She and Ned were staying on board *Ramesses*.

Alex sat at the controls of *Memphis*. "Let's get this mission underway," he said. He guided *Memphis* away from the dock and rotated the heat shield towards the planet's surface.

"Are you ready for the ride of your lives?" he asked Lem and Izzy.

They nodded, but no one knew what the next six-minute attempt to land on Mars would be like.

Memphis streaked through
the Mars atmosphere.
Outside, the heat shield was
as hot as the Sun's surface,
but inside the temperature
stayed cool.

Coconut munched on some
lettuce in her space hutch.

Four minutes later, Alex
launched the huge parachute.
It billowed out behind *Memphis*,
slowing the lander down.

"This really is a strange coloured sky," remarked Izzy. Mars was covered in an orange-red afternoon haze.

Suddenly a strong gust of wind caught *Memphis* and the lander swerved. They were right above a huge volcano. A fiery glowing lava flow oozed out of the crater below them.

"Alex, do something quickly," cried Izzy. "We're heading straight for that lava flow."

"I can't! The wind is too strong," said Alex. "We're out of control!"

Alex, Lem and Izzy were being tossed around like clothes in a washing machine.

Suddenly the wind changed direction, lifting the lander's parachute.

Memphis floated away from the danger of the main crater.

Alex regained control as the wind died down.

"Phew! Perhaps we can land more safely now."

At 15 metres above the surface, Alex fired the upward rockets. *Memphis* came to a dead stop.

The parachute detached and wheels beneath the lander lowered. Alex fired short boosts of downward rockets. *Memphis* touched down on the surface.

"*Memphis* has landed," Alex said to CapCom.

Mars Data File

Location: fourth planet from the Sun

Landscape: rocky, barren, rust red, iron-rich ground

Size: just over half the size of Earth

Length of days: 24.6 Earth hours

Length of year: 687 Earth days

Olympus Mons

The largest volcano in the solar system, Olympus Mons, is on Mars. It is wider than England and three times taller than Mount Everest, the highest mountain on Earth. It has stopped erupting.

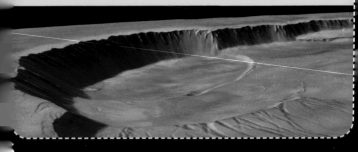

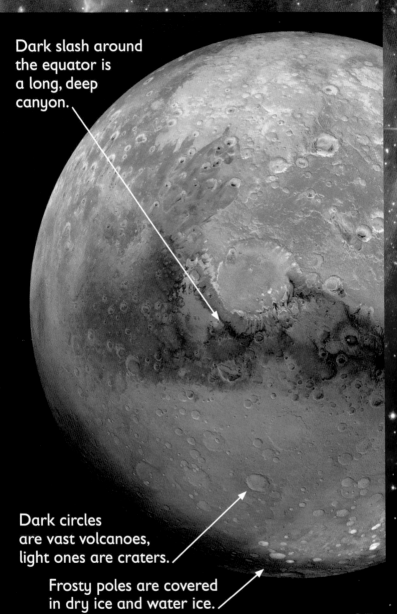

Dark slash around the equator is a long, deep canyon.

Dark circles are vast volcanoes, light ones are craters.

Frosty poles are covered in dry ice and water ice.

37

Mars Base

The astronauts' first task was to set up the base. The base was built by screwing together tubes of metal sections to form a firm structure. Solar panels for power were erected.

Satellites were set up
for communications with
Ramesses and CapCom.

Mars Phase 2
Canyon Exploration

Lem, Alex and Izzy started exploring now that the base was set up. They set off on their quad bikes specially designed for moving over the rocky Martian ground.

In a few hours, they reached the edge of the great canyon, Valles Marineris.

Alex set up the monitor equipment.

"I'm glad we have our suits on," said Alex. "The readings show high levels of carbon dioxide. We couldn't have breathed on our own in this thin air."

"We would choke on the fine dust, too," added Lem.

Try saying **Valles Marineris:** VAL-less mar-uh-NAIR-iss. At 4,000 km long and 7 km deep, the canyon is the length of the USA and seven times deeper than the Grand Canyon.

Meanwhile, Lem and Izzy
unpacked and built the glider.
Izzy strapped herself in and
switched on the video camera.

"Be careful of the strong
winds," said Lem through
the suit's radio.

Izzy lifted off and flew over the
edge. The ground dropped away
into the darkness of a deep gap.

She soared along the canyon, using the uplift of the swirling, whirling wind currents.
She swooped over the towering rocks, worn away by the wind.
She glided over giant landslides and huge sand dunes.

"That was awesome, guys!" gasped Izzy, as she landed back with Lem and Alex.

Suddenly, Alex spotted a twirling and swirling twister of dust, speeding across the canyon.

"A colossal storm is coming straight for us," said Alex. "Let's get out of here, fast."

They jumped onto the quad bikes and sped away, but the twister was catching them up.

"We're not going to make the base," cried Izzy. "We need to find some cover."

"What's that dark patch over there in the rocks?" asked Lem.

"That could be one of the Seven Sisters caves. Perfect!" called Alex.

They headed over to the cave as the twister sped closer.

As they reached the cave, they could feel the wind around their suits. They were nearly blown off the bikes. Izzy grabbed Coconut in her hutch. They all staggered to the cave opening. The darkness of the cave loomed.

Lem led the way as they entered the cave carefully.

"How far down does it go?" asked Alex, shouting over the screaming wind.

"I can't see the bottom. It could be a sheer drop," Lem shouted.

"There's a slight ledge with enough space for us to shelter," suggested Izzy.

The storm whistled past the cave entrance. Pieces of dust and rocks were thrown into the cave. They just missed the cowering astronauts.

As the wind died down, Izzy, Lem and Alex were able to look around them.

"There are tunnels that go much further back," said Alex.

"Hey, guys," said Lem, excitedly. "There are markings on the walls."

"That's strange?" queried Izzy.
"The markings look more like
a fossil of a skeleton."

"Mmm-martians from the past?"
whispered Lem in surprise.

They looked at each other,
quizzically.

Make Some Martian Spacedust

To make some Martian dust, you will need some sand, a tray, washing-up gloves, scissors, wire wool and water.

1 Half-fill the tray with sand. Wearing gloves, cut the wire wool into pieces and mix it into the sand. Wet the sand. Leave the tray uncovered in a safe place.

2 Check the sand every day and add more water if it dries out. Wait for the sand to turn a rusty red colour due to the wire wool and water.

Mars dust facts

1 The soil on Mars is red because it contains large quantities of iron. The grey rocks are coated with this bright red dust.

2 Scientists believe that water did once flow on the surface of Mars, but now just the air contains water vapour.

3 It never rains on Mars because the planet is very cold, so it is dry and dusty like a desert. Any water on its surface would turn to ice or vapour.

4 A dust devil is a twirling wind like a mini-tornado that picks up dust as it speeds along.

5 Dust storms can cover the whole planet and last for a few days. These are caused by the Sun warming the atmosphere and causing the air to move, lifting the dust off the surface.

North Pole

For the next few days, the astronauts were unable to leave the base. They had received warnings from Mission Control of a solar flare. These extra strong rays of the Sun could kill them because the Martian atmosphere would not protect them as Earth's does.

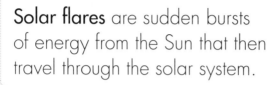

Solar flares are sudden bursts of energy from the Sun that then travel through the solar system.

Finally, CapCom gave them the all clear.

Lem, Izzy and Alex set off eagerly on their quad bikes. This time they headed for the North Pole. They had changed the bikes' wheels to the ones that could grip on sand dunes. It took them over half the day to cover the distance.

Alex set up the monitors straight away to measure the depth of the dry ice.

"It's like stepping through clouds," remarked Izzy.

"It's hard to get any grip," said Lem, as he struggled to climb an arch-shaped sand dune. He slid back with each step he took.

"I'm not surprised. There's a layer of slippery sand and dust below this dry ice," replied Izzy.

Mars is very cold. The **North Pole** is covered by dry ice and water ice. Dry ice is frozen carbon dioxide.

"Guys, come and take a look at this water ice sample under the microscope," said Alex, excitedly. "I've melted it and found some tiny creatures."

Lem peered into the microscope to see the wriggling creatures.

"Wow! You've unfrozen
the Martians," laughed Lem.
Coconut in her space hutch
looked interested, too.
"Keep your whiskers out of
the way," laughed Izzy.

Asteroids [AS-ter-oids] are space rocks. There is a ring of millions of asteroids between Mars and the next outer planet, Jupiter.

Suddenly the CapCom radio beeped.

"Hey guys! There's an asteroid coming your way. We estimate impact will be in less than twelve hours. You need to get off Mars and back to *Ramesses* NOW."

"Message received and understood," said Lem, urgently. "We'll head back to *Memphis* straight away."

Alex clung on to his samples as the team sped back to base.

Without delay, they climbed into *Memphis*. Izzy placed Coconut safely inside her hutch in the hold.

Alex sat at the controls and fired up the booster rockets. *Memphis* rumbled as it lifted off the red planet.

On *Ramesses*, Flo and Ned were ready to meet them.

"Welcome back," they cried, as Alex, Lem and Izzy appeared through the hatch.

"And just in time!" said Flo.

"The asteroid hit Mars a few minutes ago and left a big crater."

"Mission Control has given us the go-ahead to continue the mission," said Ned, pleased. "Next stop, Jupiter!"

Space Quest Quiz

1. What colour are the astronaut's launch suits?

2. How does the landing capsule slow down to land safely?

3. How many Earth days makes a year on Mars?

4. Why is the soil on Mars red?

5. Why did Lem, Izzy and Alex need to leave Mars quickly?

Answers on page 64.

Glossary

atmosphere
layer of gas
surrounding
a planet

capsule
small spacecraft as
part of a larger one

comet
ball of icy rock,
frozen gas and
spacedust with
a tail of gas
and dust

freeze-dried food
food that is quickly
frozen and dried
for storing

harnessed
strapped in

impact
hitting hard

intercept
stop or interrupt
a journey

microscope
scientific instrument
that makes very
small things
appear bigger

orbit
curved path around
a planet or a star

sample
small collection
of something
for studying

vapour
moisture in the air
that can be seen,
such as steam

Guide for Parents

DK Reads is a three-level interactive reading adventure series for children, developing the habit of reading widely for both pleasure and information. These chapter books have an exciting main narrative interspersed with a range of reading genres to suit your child's reading ability, as required by the National Curriculum. Each book is designed to develop your child's reading skills, fluency, grammar awareness, and comprehension in order to build confidence and engagement when reading.

Ready for a *Starting to Read Alone* book

YOUR CHILD SHOULD

- be able to read most words without needing to stop and break them down into sound parts.

- read smoothly, in phrases and with expression.
  By this level, your child will be mostly reading silently.

- self-correct when some word or sentence doesn't sound right.

A VALUABLE AND SHARED READING EXPERIENCE

For some children, text reading, particularly non-fiction, requires much effort but adult participation can make this both fun and easier. So here are a few tips on how to use this book with your child.

TIP 1 Check out the contents together before your child begins:

- invite your child to check the blurb, contents page and layout of the book and comment on it.

- ask your child to make predictions about the story.

- chat about the information your child might want to find out.

TIP 2 Encourage fluent and flexible reading:

- support your child to read in fluent, expressive phrases, making full use of punctuation and thinking about the meaning.

* encourage your child to slow down and check information where appropriate.

TIP 3 Indicators that your child is reading for meaning:

* your child will be responding to the text if he/she is self-correcting and varying his/her voice.

* your child will want to chat about what he/she is reading or is eager to turn the page to find out what will happen next.

TIP 4 Praise, share and chat:

* the factual pages tend to be more difficult than the story pages, and are designed to be shared with your child.

* encourage your child to recall specific details after each chapter.

* provide opportunities for your child to pick out interesting words and discuss what they mean.

* discuss how the author captures the reader's interest, or how effective the non-fiction layouts are.

* ask questions about the text. These help to develop comprehension skills and awareness of the language used.

A FEW ADDITIONAL TIPS

* Read to your child regularly to demonstrate fluency, phrasing and expression; to find out or check information; and for sharing enjoyment.

* Encourage your child to reread favourite texts to increase reading confidence and fluency.

* Check that your child is reading a range of different types, such as poems, jokes and following instructions.

Series consultant **Shirley Bickler** is a longtime advocate of carefully crafted, enthralling texts for young readers. Her LIFT initiative for infant teaching was the model for the National Literacy Strategy Literacy Hour, and she is co-author of *Book Bands for Guided Reading* published by Reading Recovery based at the Institute of Education.

Index

Answers to the Space Quest Quiz:

1. Orange; **2.** Uses a parachute; **3.** 687 Earth days; **4.** Contains iron; **5.** An asteroid would hit Mars.